# Time For Bed, Baby

## By Tanya Leary

## Illustrated by Lisa Williams

Copyright 2018

First Published 2018

ISBN 978-1978008793

**TEAMAUTHOR** TA UK
*Publishing with you*

## Dedication:

For Bethan Gwen & Hannah Muriel.
I will love you until the seas run dry;
And that will never happen.

Always be true to you.

Muma.
X

# About This Book

When you become a parent, it is easy to be overwhelmed; by emotions, by advice from books and websites and well-meaning individuals.
**That's natural.**
You are raising a whole new human being – it is a big deal and it can seem scary!

This book was written for you by someone that has been overwhelmed by all of those things at some point (and still is!) My hope is that this verse will act as a tool to remind you to make time and take time to just be and appreciate that you honestly are doing a good job.

No matter how it may look, no one gets it right all the time.
There isn't a "one size fits all" way to parent; it is part of what makes us and our babies so unique and precious.

This bedtime sequence and book is partly an end-of-day relaxation routine, part love story to mums and babies everywhere.

It is intended to help you carve out a space at the end of each day; whether it has been all sunshine and sparkles or more tears and tantrums. Be in the moment with your baby; notice the sensation of the bath water and bubbles, marvel at their tiny fingers and toes, and breathe in their precious smell.

Let this book serve as a daily reminder that you are doing your best and you are enough. You really are.

### Much Love.
### X

This is your bath
and these are the bubbles.

When you are washed
I will give you some cuddles.

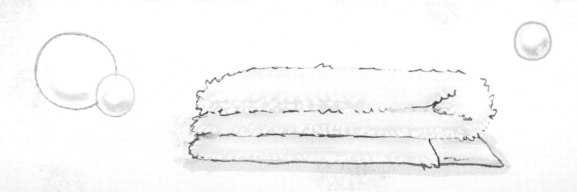

These are your cheeks
and this is your nose.

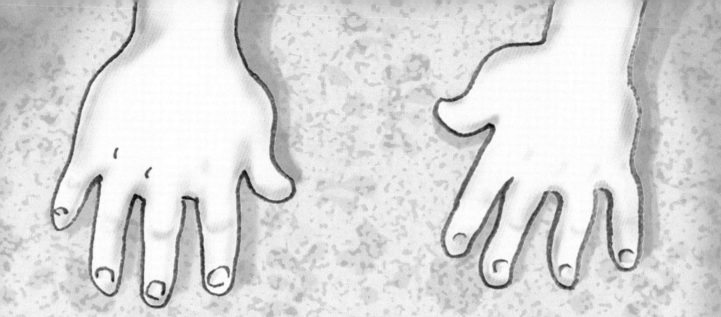

These are your fingers
and these are your toes.

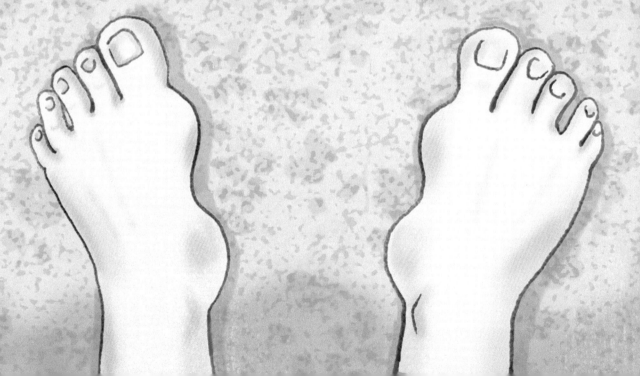

This is your tummy
and this is your head.

It's time to get out
and get ready for bed.

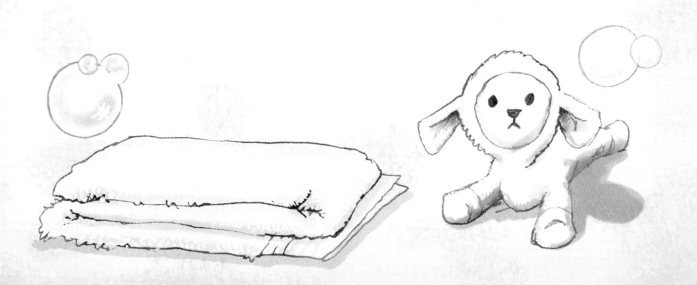

This is your dolly
and this is your duck.

This is your towel
and here is your hug.

These are your jim jams
and here is your milk.

Let's brush your hair,
it feels just like silk.

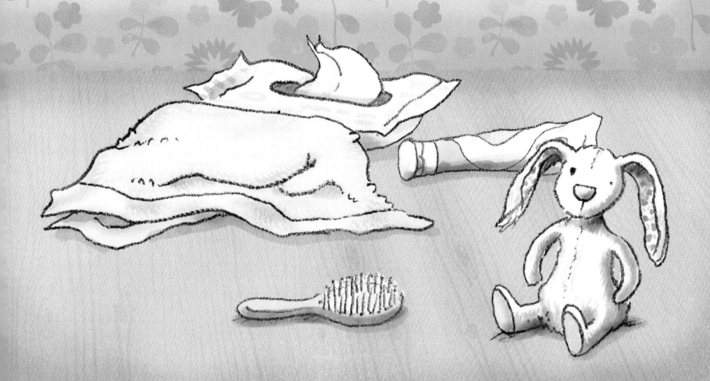

# This is your teddy and this is your bed.

# This is a safe place for resting your head

This is your mobile

and this is
your light.

And I am your mummy
kissing you goodnight.

You are loved.

Always.

Sleep tight xx

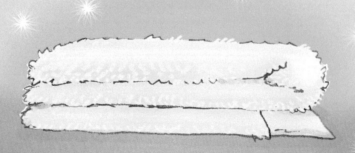

# Acknowledgements

There are so many people that have not only helped me to get this book to print but have helped me carry on 'mumming' when I didn't feel I could.
Their love, support and endless encouragement mean so much.

Thank you to the whole team at Team Author UK, to Clare from LushTums and to my beautiful friends and family – without you, I am not me.

**Thank you.**

www.lushtums.co.uk

## Time for You

Too often the idea of mums taking time out just for us is seen as self-indulgent and too often that message comes mainly from ourselves.

The following yoga and relaxation sequence has been put together especially for this publication by Clare Maddalena, founder of LushTums - the UK's leading experts in birth preparation, pregnancy yoga, postnatal yoga and classes for children and their grown ups.

It is about giving yourself a space at the end of the day to allow yourself time to relax, recharge and let go of whatever has come before that moment, so you are ready to give again tomorrow.

# Alternate Nostril Breathing

This is an amazing de-stresser and anxiety reducer, helping us to focus on the present moment, letting go of what has come before as well as future worries. Ideal for clearing your head after a busy day.

Sit tall (either in a chair or cross-legged on the floor) with your hands relaxed in your lap. You can bring the index finger and thumb to lightly touch. Close your eyes if possible or have a soft gaze and try to consciously relax your face and soften your shoulders. Keep your breathing slow and deep and take the deepest breaths you can into your tummy.

As you breathe, concentrate on one nostril at a time; you'll actually breathe in through both, but with focus you can feel more on one side and then the other.

Try this: really feel the right nostril as you breathe in. Feel the breath coming in and up the right nostril. Then exhale down the left nostril, really feel the left nostril. Then breathe back up the left side, and nostril, feeling as much as you can. Then exhale down the right side.

Breathe back up the right side, feel the breath come right up into your head.

Exhale down the left and feel the breath come right down into your sit bone.
Inhale back up the left side of your body and nostril.
Exhale down the right, all the way to your sit bone.

Keep going in this rhythm for between 2-3 minutes. When you finish, end on exhaling down the left side.

or

in through your right

out through your left

# Moving the Spine and Opening Your Chest

When you've been carrying a bump around for what feels like an eternity and then carrying a baby, your back can take a bit of a battering. Add in the posture of feeding and by the end of the day, you can feel as if each vertebra is compacting on top of one another. Not good! I love this sequence; it really opens me back up and feels like it gives me back an inch or so in height!

## Sitting Cat/Cow

Sit on the floor in easy pose with your hands on your knees. As you inhale, arch your back in an exaggerated fashion and as you exhale, round your back, like a cat. As you warm up, try to increase the range of movement gently to really show your spine some love. Repeat 8-10 times.

Breathe out, chin on chest, and arch the back

Lift

Breathe in, flex and arch the back

# Shoulder and Chest Openers

As I am typing, I am actually pausing to do these exercises so whether you are working or nursing (or neither), these are excellent for anyone.

Bring your hands to your heart in prayer pose and as you inhale, raise your arms up over your head and then roll your shoulders back and down.

*inhale and reach up*

*Exhale, arms out and down*

# Side Bend

This massages our internal organs and is really energising. As you breathe in, lift up and over and exhale as you return to centre.

*Reach up & over*

*Then repeat on other side*

# Gentle Twist

This is best if you do this on your knees as it helps to keep the spine nice and straight. As you inhale, grow as tall as you can, balance out your shoulders and then, as you exhale, twist and look gently over your shoulder, being careful to do this gently.

*look behind you, keep shoulders look*

*or, sit tall,*

*then turn to look behid you*

# Resting Heart
## (or Legs up the Wall pose!)

This is my kind of pose: quick and simple but gives a brilliant boost in next to no time! Perfect pre school run!

Allowing the blood to flow back towards the heart and brain really nourishes your internal organs and enables your heart to rest and slow down. 5 to 10 minutes of this is utter bliss.

Wriggle your bottom as close to a wall as possible and then simply rest your legs softly against the wall and breathe.

Ahhh!

Rest
5-10 minutes
chin in

Relaxed legs
& feet

You can use a
small pillow for
comfort

## Relaxation

Zoning out, switching off and really trying to take some time out can be tricky but I honestly, honestly believe that this is one of the single, most important things that you can do to look after you and, in turn your baby and your family. If you have people around you offering to help or to have the baba for an hour or so – take them up on it; it is part of what keeps me sane. Genuinely!

Time for you might mean a walk, a run, a drink with friends, a bath and a book, a coffee and cake in blissful silence OR...listening to a gorgeous meditation download. Happily, Clare and the team at LushTums have created this fantastic free download for exactly this purpose.

## ENJOY!

Download direct from the LushTums website free of charge using the code:

TIMEFORBED

www.lushtums.co.uk/relaxation-quests
/mamas-self-care-quest

## About the Author

Tanya is a storyteller who enjoys nothing more than snuggling up with a book, a blanket and her babies. She believes that snuggles, stories, kisses and kindness have the power to change the world and as such, should be shared as widely as possible.
Tanya lives on the Wirral with her husband and family.

◎ 🐦 @mumaleary

mummetamorphosis.wordpress.com

## About the Illustrator

Lisa Williams decided to be an illustrator whilst she was still in primary school. She has been illustrating children's books, magazines and educational material for nearly 25 years.

Lisa is one of the illustrators for TeamAuthorUK.

For more information visit Lisa's Facebook page:

Facebook.com/lisawilliamsillustration

Made in the USA
Lexington, KY
25 June 2018